Girls Play Hockey Too!

by Kimberly Jo Simac

Illustrations by Emily Rose Gritt

This book is dedicated to our mothers
Susan and Lynell
who have always believed in our dreams.
Love, Kim and Emily

A special thank you to:
Kitty Sookochoff
Matt Van Skyhawk
Jason Neubauer
Dara Maillette
Abbey Maillette

Published by
Great Northern Adventure Co., Inc.
3860 Kula Vista Drive - P.O. Box 961
Eagle River, WI 54521
715-479-8784
bk951@verizon.net
www.gnaco.com

Layout and Editing by:
Great Northern Adventure Co., Inc.
Abbey Maillette
Dara Maillette

Photography by:
Lakeside Studios
Kitty Sookochoff
715-479-2974
www.lakesidephoto.com

Printing Managed by
RR Donnelley
Menasha, Wisconsin

Library of Congress Cataloging-in-Publication Data
Simac, Kimberly Jo

ISBN-978-0-9763931-1-5

ISBN-0-9763931-1-5

Printed in China
1st Printing

To girls who

dream of hockey...

I got my first skates
when I was two.
It was Christmas time,
and the box was blue.

It was not easy,
but I learned
to skate.

By the end of the year,
I was really great!

When I was five,
I could spin and twirl.
My new skates
were the color of pearls.

I skated each day
and worked very hard.
I knew that someday
I would be a star.

I skated each year in the famous ice show
I was a flower, a clown,
and a box with a bow.

I learned how to skate backwards
and stop very fast.
I really loved skating, and I had a blast!

I learned how to play hockey
on the floor of the lobby.

In a very short time,
it was my favorite hobby.

It was fun to catch a pass,
skate the puck up and score.

Figure skating was fun,
but I liked hockey even more.

I told my parents
that it was my dream...

...to get my own gear,
and try out for a team.

My Dad laughed and said hockey was for boys.

Mom shook her head and said I should stick to dolls and toys.

I tried to tell them
that it was not true.

I told them there are lots
of girls who play hockey too!

So I practiced all summer
on my roller blades.

I got faster and stronger,
and more determined
to play.

I told my Mom
that hockey
was for me.

That I could even
shoot better
than some of
the boys
on the team.

She shrugged
her shoulders,
as if she
did not care.

Somehow,
it just didn't
seem very fair.

My birthday
was coming
and all I wished for
were new hockey skates
and gear
from the sports store.

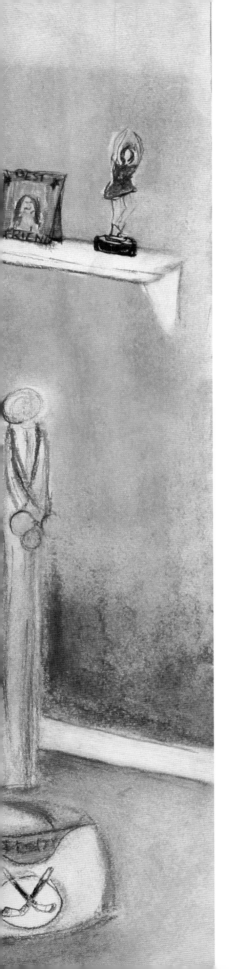

On the morning
of my birthday
I woke up to find
a hockey bag by my bed
with a helmet inside.

There were
new skates, gloves,
breezers, pads,
and more.

There was even
a brand new stick
leaning next
to the door.

I jumped for
joy and yelled

"HOORAY!"

"I am playing hockey
starting today!"

Now I play hockey,
like lots of girls do.

Hockey is the BEST,
and it really is true.